STORIES FOR
7 YEAR OLDS

A Random House book
Published by Random House Australia Pty Ltd
Level 3, 100 Pacific Highway, North Sydney NSW 2060
www.randomhouse.com.au

First published by Random House Australia in 2014

National Library of Australia
Cataloguing-in-Publication Entry

Title: Stories for seven year olds/edited by Linsay Knight
ISBN: 978 0 85798 479 1 (pbk)
Target audience: For primary school age.
Subject: Children's stories, Australian.
Other authors/contributors:
   Knight, Linsay, editor
   Jellett, Tom, illustrator
Dewey number: A823.01089282

Cover illustration by Tom Jellett
Cover design by Leanne Beattie
Internal design and typesetting by Midland Typesetters, Australia
Printed in Australia by Griffin Press, an accredited ISO AS/NZS
14001:2004 Environmental Management System printer

Random House Australia uses papers that are natural, renewable and
recyclable products and made from wood grown in sustainable forests.
The logging and manufacturing processes are expected to conform to the
environmental regulations of the country of origin.

STORIES FOR
7 YEAR OLDS

Stories by
**BELINDA MURRELL, BILL CONDON,
JACQUELINE HARVEY AND MORE!**

Edited by
LINSAY KNIGHT

Illustrated by
TOM JELLETT

RANDOM HOUSE AUSTRALIA

FOREWORD

BACK BY POPULAR DEMAND!

What a treat it is to search for the special stories that tickle children's tastebuds and find a treasured place on their burgeoning reading menus, to be sampled again and again. This collection showcases these stories in order to excite seven-year-old readers, enable them to test their growing skills and continue their reading adventure in a safe and reassuring environment. And that's why we have also given such careful consideration to the reading requirements of this age group, such as content, author style and voice, as well as the ratio of text to illustration and type size.

The large, clear type and imaginative black-line illustrations by Tom Jellett encourage these emerging readers to move from reading aloud to an adult or older child to confident silent reading, while the short episodic chapters or scenes keep the reader hooked.

These stories take emerging readers into worlds beyond the familiar – to fantastical and humorous worlds. A narrative style and first-person narrator, who speaks directly to the readers, are often used. This helps to draw them immediately into the action.

The second of four specially selected collections, *Stories for 7 Year Olds* includes offerings from the following inspirational Australian storytellers: Belinda Murrell, Bill Condon, Celeste Walters, David Harding, Fiona McDonald, Grace Atwood, George Ivanoff, Sophie Masson, Vashti Farrer, Goldie Alexander, Jenny Blackford and Jacqueline Harvey.

We are proud to present such a friendly and accessible book, essential for children who adore being read to and demand a good read.

– Linsay Knight

CONTENTS

LULU BELL AND THE BEACH ADVENTURE

BY BELINDA MURRELL

It was a five-minute walk from Shelly Beach school to the sheltered cove beach. The sun danced on the blue water of the harbour. It glinted and glittered. Dazzling white sailboats skimmed across the water and a ferry honked its horn. Seagulls swooped and soared, squabbling for scraps. The air smelt of salt and seaweed and hot chips.

1

Lulu Bell pulled off her hot shoes and socks. She squelched the crumbly sand between her toes.

Mum made a screen of beach towels. The children took turns to duck behind the towels and wriggle into their swimming costumes and rash vests. Mum slathered them all with sunscreen.

'Race you in,' called Lulu. She threw her hat on her bag and set off towards the water. Her best friend Molly and little sister Rosie squealed and chased her. They splashed through the tiny waves on the shore.

The water was cold and clear and wonderful. It washed away the stickiness of the day. The girls dived and dunked, catching each other by the heel.

Lulu's little brother, Gus, ran into the water, still wearing his Bug Boy costume. He jumped into the shallows and shrieked with glee.

The sun was sinking on the western horizon. It streaked the sky with brilliant hues of crimson, gold and purple.

Lulu, Rosie, Gus and Molly explored the rock pools. They peered at crabs and periwinkles. They poked at sea anemones with their fingers to make them close up.

'Lulu,' called Mum. 'Rosie, Gus. It's time to go home.'

Mum packed up. The children dried off and put on their school uniforms. Their skin felt crusty with salt and sand and fun.

'If we're very lucky we might see a fairy penguin,' said Mum. 'They have a colony in this cove. Their burrows are at the foot of those cliffs and under the wharf. They go out fishing all day and come back at dusk.'

'We learned about the penguins at school,' said Lulu. 'Miss Baxter said they don't call them fairy penguins anymore – they call them little penguins.'

'I know,' said Mum. 'But I love the name fairy penguins. It seems to suit them.'

Everyone started walking towards the fish and chip shop on the wharf. Lulu suddenly felt hungry. It had been a long afternoon of swimming, running and playing. Her tummy rumbled at the thought of crunchy, hot fish and salty, crispy chips. *Yum.*

'Look,' said Rosie. 'Is that a fairy penguin?'

Everyone craned their heads to see where Rosie was pointing. Among the dim shadows, the waves broke on the beach. A darker shadow was waddling up the sand.

'Yes,' said Lulu. 'I think it is. Can we go down and look at it?'

'No, honey bun,' replied Mum. 'You can look from here. The penguins are wild animals. You need to stay well away or you'll frighten them. He's probably on his way home to feed a nest full of baby chicks.'

'Ooh,' cried Lulu. 'I'd like to see them.'

The four children clustered at the

side of the footpath. The penguin
waddled faster, heading away from
the water.

A noise made Lulu look up. Coming
towards them was a scruffy dog. It was
running wildly and dragging a boy
behind it.

Suddenly, the boy tripped on a bump
in the footpath and sprawled face first on
the ground. He dropped the leash and
the dog bounded away. The boy started
crying.

'Lulu, see if you can catch that dog,'
called Mum. She hurried to help the
fallen boy. 'There now, sweetie, have you
hurt yourself?'

The boy had a nasty graze on his left
knee. He had more on his left elbow and

on his chin. The grazes oozed blood,
which made the boy cry louder.

The dog had jumped down onto the
beach. It yapped with delight as it raced
towards the little penguin.

Lulu and Molly sprinted down the
stairs to the beach. The penguin waddled
faster.

'Good dog,' coaxed Lulu. 'Come on,
boy. Come here.'

The dog took no notice. It jumped
on the penguin and knocked it over. The
dog yapped and woofed. Then it tossed
the penguin in the air with its snout.

'No,' screamed Lulu. She ran faster. 'Bad dog. Stop that at once.'

The penguin squeaked with terror. The dog picked the seabird up in its mouth and dropped it again like a toy.

Lulu reached the dog and grabbed its trailing lead. She dragged the dog away. The little penguin stayed huddled on the sand.

'Bad dog,' she cried. 'Molly, can you hold the dog for me, please?'

Molly took the lead. She strained to hold the bouncy dog back.

'He's strong!' complained Molly.

Lulu dropped to her knees in the sand. She was careful not to touch the little bird. It was breathing heavily. Tears filled her eyes so she could hardly see.

Mum came racing across the sand.
Rosie and Gus followed.

'Is it okay?' asked Mum.

'I don't know,' hiccuped Lulu.

The penguin was making low
squeaking sounds. Lulu couldn't see any
outward signs of injury. The dog yapped,
lurching and trying to escape.

'I think the penguin is in shock.'
Mum rummaged in her handbag and
pulled out her phone. She passed it to
Lulu. 'Lulu, can you call Dad, please?
Tell him what's happened and ask him
to come at once.'

Mum helped Molly pull the dog away
and made everyone stand back.

Lulu dialled her dad's number.
Her fingers were shaky. Lulu's dad was

a vet. Lulu's family lived right behind the Shelly Beach Vet Hospital.

'Hi, Dad,' said Lulu. Her voice wobbled. 'It's me. We're down at the cove. A dog attacked a little penguin. It might be injured. Mum says can you come straight away?'

'Of course, sweetie, I'm on my way. Where exactly are you?' asked Dad.

The sound of Dad's familiar, confident voice made Lulu feel better. Dad would know what to do. Dad would make the penguin better.

'On the beach, near the wharf,' replied Lulu. 'We were going to get fish and chips.'

'Don't worry – just make sure no one touches the penguin. I'll be there soon,' said Dad.

The rest of the group had gathered around Mum and the dog. There was Rosie, Gus, Molly, Finn – the boy who'd fallen over – and now his mother.

'Dad's coming,' said Lulu.

Mum brushed Lulu's hair back and kissed her on the forehead. 'Good work, honey bun,' said Mum. 'You've done well.'

'Scruffy, you bad, bad dog,' said Finn's mother.

'My husband is a vet and he's on his way,' explained Mum. 'I think we should go up on the footpath and wait for him there. Lulu, perhaps you and Molly could wait here with the penguin. Make sure he stays safe.'

Molly and Lulu squatted on the damp sand. The penguin lay still, a dark hump on the paler sand. Lulu could see her mum up above the seawall. She was talking to the others.

'It'll be okay, little fella,' murmured Lulu. 'My dad will be here soon.'

———

In a few minutes, Lulu spied the familiar sight of her tall, gangly dad. He was carrying his black medical bag and a cardboard box. Lulu ran towards him.

'Dad! Dad! It's over here,' called Lulu.

Dad swooped her up over his head and kissed her. 'That's my precious girl,' he said. 'Show me this little penguin of yours.'

Dad ran his hands carefully over the penguin. He listened to its heartbeat with his stethoscope. Carefully, he lifted

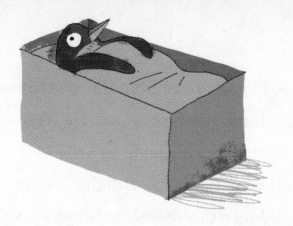

the bird. He wrapped it in an old towel
and tucked it into the cardboard box.

'I think this little guy is coming home
with us,' said Dad. He hoisted the box
and tucked it under one arm. 'He's in a
bit of shock.'

'Do you think he'll be okay?' asked
Lulu. Her voice wobbled again.

Dad gave her a squeeze with his free
arm. 'I think he'll be fine,' he replied.

Lulu's dad had driven from the vet
hospital to the beach. Mum had found
the car and packed all the gear into the

boot. Finn and his mother were waiting with Mum.

'I'm so sorry,' said Finn's mother. 'Will the penguin be all right?'

'I think so,' replied Dad, 'but he's a lucky bird. I'm glad that Lulu and Molly stopped Scruffy. In another few minutes the penguin could have been dead.'

———

In the consulting room, Dad lifted the bird out of the box. The penguin yelped and flapped his dark flippers in protest. His silver-grey eyes blinked rapidly in the bright light.

'He's a noisy little fellow,' said Dad. 'That's a good sign.'

Lulu smiled with relief.

'Look, Lulu,' said Dad. 'His back is blue-grey to make him hard to see from the sky. And his tummy is white. That's so he looks like foam from underneath the water. Isn't that clever?'

'It is,' agreed Lulu. 'He's really cute.'

Dad checked the bird closely. He moved its flippers gently and ran his hands over the feathers.

'Can you pass me that tube, please, sweetie? It's antibiotic ointment,' said Dad. 'There's a slight graze on his side.'

Lulu handed Dad the tube and he smeared the graze with ointment.

'Nothing's broken,' Dad decided, 'but I think he's suffering from shock and bruising. I'll give him a shot of antibiotics. Then we'll take him back to the cove and release him.'

'Oh, no,' said Lulu. 'Can't we keep him, at least for a few days?'

'Sweetie, this little guy probably has a mate. She will be worried about him. Plus she'll have a burrow full of little chicks. They will be hungry,' explained Dad. 'You know, if Scruffy had killed this penguin, all his chicks could have died as well. The chicks need one parent to stay and look after them. The other parent goes out hunting for food.'

Lulu nodded. 'Then of course he needs to go home,' she agreed.

'Do you want to come with me to let him go?' asked Dad.

'Yes please, Dad.'

Lulu held the box on her lap as Dad drove back to the cove. She could feel the penguin moving around inside. He squeaked and yelped. He smelt fishy.

Dad parked the car near the wharf and came around to open the door for Lulu. He lifted the box off her lap so she could climb out. The beach was completely dark now. Only the footpath was lit by streetlights.

'Can I carry him, please?' Lulu asked.

'Sure, sweetie. Just be careful not to drop him.'

Slowly and carefully, Lulu carried the box down the steps and onto the beach.

'I think we'll let him go right where you found him,' said Dad.

Their eyes slowly adjusted to the darkness. Lulu could just see the scuff marks from the struggle in the damp sand.

She knelt down and placed the box on the sand. Dad slowly turned the box on its side and opened the lid. The penguin paused for a moment. Then he scuttled out of the box. He ran up the sand towards his burrow under the jetty.

'Welcome home,' murmured Lulu. 'Sleep well, little penguin.'

THAT'S SHOWBIZ

BY BILL CONDON

My second best friend Jenny Tong
wants to be a world-famous doctor who
discovers a cure for something really
terrible, like warts.

I want to be a star, but I'm not a
very good actor. My only role so far was
in a play called *The Quiet Boy*. I played
a super-shy kid who hardly ever said
a word.

I'm usually pretty quiet, but not that
time. I got the giggles all through the
first act. I got the hiccups in the second
act. I don't think it was meant to be a

funny play but the audience laughed.

That was a year ago. Now, here I am again, trying out for a new play. Our teacher, Mr Spinoza, chooses the cast.

Jenny and Tricia are trees.

Magnus and Elly are rocks. So is Mike.

Carlos and Denise are the back end of a dragon.

Maria and Costas are the front end.

Bruno is Wally the Wicked Gnome.

There are also about ten kids in the chorus. Whenever the dragon is coming, they have to yell: 'Here comes the dragon!'

I think Mr Spinoza has forgotten me, so I bob up and down, waving my hands.

'Ah, David,' he says. 'I have the perfect role for you.'

'Am I the star?' I ask.

'Not this time. You're a giant mushroom.'

'Huh? Why am I a mushroom?'

Mike digs me in the ribs. 'Because you look like a mushroom. And you smell like one too!'

I am not impressed.

Mr Spinoza points at Carmela. 'You can play the part of Princess Darla.'

Carmela's face turns so red it looks like her brain has exploded.

Next, he points at Tony Bosco. Tony's got a photographic memory – but he doesn't only remember photos. He remembers everything!

'You can play the part of Prince Roger,' says Mr Spinoza.

'Okay,' Tony replies, as if it's no big deal.

Now he's a star, and I'm a mushroom. Oh, well, that's showbiz.

Mr Spinoza sits on a desk and kicks his legs up and down as he explains the play. 'It's called *The Prince and the Dragon*,' he says. 'It's about a prince who sets out to save a beautiful princess.'

Carmela grins. 'That's me!'

'As I was saying, Prince Roger wants to rescue Princess Darla, but she's held prisoner in a castle by Wally the Wicked Gnome.'

Bruno – alias Wally – cackles wickedly.

'The castle is guarded by a fire-breathing dragon,' Mr Spinoza adds.

Both ends of the dragon clap their hands. 'That's us!'

'What do the trees do?' asks Jenny.

'And the rocks?' adds Magnus.

Very loudly, I ask, 'What about the mushroom?'

Mr Spinoza says they all come alive and try to stop Prince Roger from saving Princess Darla.

I like that idea. The trees and rocks and the giant mushroom will jump on Tony and squash him. Good fun.

'Of course,' Mr Spinoza adds, 'the Prince easily defeats you.'

I hate that idea.

———

For the first couple of rehearsals everything goes fine. We know our lines. We're having lots of fun. Mr Spinoza smiles all the time.

But then we're given our costumes. They're really smelly and tatty. The dragon costume looks about a hundred years old. As soon as they put it on, the back end of the dragon gets hay fever.

Carlos erupts with a thunderous 'Aaa-chooo!'

Denise blows her nose with a huge 'Honnnkk!'

The front end of the dragon gets itchy.

Costas pokes his head out. 'Something's biting me.'

'Fleas!' yells Maria. 'This dragon's got fleas!'

'Aaa-chooo!'

'Honnnkk!'

Carlos, Denise, Maria and Costas wriggle out of their dragon costume and start jumping on it to kill the fleas.

Mr Spinoza's itching, too. The fleas have hopped onto his ankle. Now they're on his leg. Now they're attacking his bottom!

———

The costumes are sent away to be washed. We keep on rehearsing without them. It's not so much fun anymore. Some kids complain, especially Bruno.

'Why do I have to be a wicked gnome?' he says. 'Why can't I be a giant?'

'You're the wicked gnome,' Mr Spinoza says. 'And that's final.'

'But I'm too nice to be wicked,' Bruno insists.

Mike grins. 'I can be wicked. Watch this!'

He pushes over Bruno's bag.

'Hey!'

He knocks off Jenny's hat.

'Don't!'

He unties Maria's shoelace.

'Go away!'

The rocks and the trees play chasings.

Mr Spinoza gets a headache.

———

We rehearse after school twice a week. But at the end of a month, instead of getting better, we get worse.

About half of the chorus is saying, 'Here comes the dragon.' The other half is saying, 'There goes the dragon.' Sometimes Kylie says, 'Here comes the elephant.' (She loves elephants.)

Bruno is still being a nice wicked gnome.

Carmel has a bad cold.

Some of the rocks and the trees are so bored they're falling asleep.

The costumes come back really clean, but Mr Spinoza makes us wait until two days before the play opens before we try them on. He thinks we'll get them dirty. But when we finally get to wear them, there's a big problem.

'I'm stuck!'

'This is too tight!'

'This can't be my costume!'

'Oh no!' groans Mr Spinoza. 'They've shrunk!'

'What will we do?'

'Don't worry,' he says. 'I'll think of something.'

———

Mr Spinoza claps his hands. 'I've got a brilliant idea!' He races to the storeroom. We all follow.

He opens a huge chest and digs through it.

'Treasure! We've got treasure!' Mr Spinoza tips over the chest and out falls a jumbled heap of masks.

They're the coolest and creepiest masks ever. Monster masks!

'They were used in a Halloween play,' says Mr Spinoza.

Tony puts on a mask. He looks like Count Dracula. 'Boo!'

Carmela puts on one, too. 'Grrrr!'

Now everyone's excited about the play.

———

At last the big day arrives.

We're scared and nervous.

'You'll be great,' says Mr Spinoza.

We perform the play exactly as
we rehearsed it, but instead of being
rocks and trees and mushrooms, we're
monsters who boo and growl and try to
scare each other.

Sometimes we forget our lines, but
that doesn't matter because the audience
can't understand us very well with the
masks on.

At the end of the play our parents
clap and cheer.

Afterwards, the Principal shakes
Mr Spinoza's hand. 'Excellent play,'
she says. 'Lots of fun. Wonderful idea
to use the masks.'

Mr Spinoza looks proud. 'I had a
great cast,' he says. 'Every one of them is
a star.'

LITTLE LAMBCHOPS

BY CELESTE WALTERS

I'm off to Pop's farm for a week on my
own. Though if you count Pop and the
manager and the manager's wife and
the shearers and the harvesters and the
hundred million cows and bulls and ewes
and rams – and Toby the dog – I won't
be on my own for long.

At last everything's packed. I have
enough stuff to go hiking in the
Himalayas for six months. I elbow legs
and arms through clothes and food and

bottles of sunscreen and squashable hats to get into the car, and we're off.

In a wink it's goodbye city and hello paddocks and white sheep and black cattle. Hello, farmhouse with a red roof. Hello, men riding tractors and boy on a horse.

After four long hours, I spot the sign for Elm Park. We swing through the gate and rattle down the drive, bumping along to Dad's moaning about having to spend next weekend cleaning the car.

Pop's waiting for us on the verandah. 'The kettle's on,' he yells.

While the grown-ups drink tea and get stuck into Mum's cake, I wander around looking for a snake or some other crawly to keep me company.

A big yawn later, with soppy kisses and warnings about being too friendly with anything with four legs, they're off.

'Well,' says Pop.

'Well,' I say.

'Come and dump your stuff.'

I love Pop talk. It goes with trudging inside with your boots on and making dirt marks on the lino.

'Eat everything?' Pop's asking.

'Um . . .' I suddenly remember how much I hate pumpkin.

'Well, there's chop, peas an' mash; sausage, peas an' mash; fish fingers, peas an' mash . . .'

I wonder how you can mash sausage. 'Pumpkin?'

'That's for the birds,' replies Pop.

This is all so cool.

'Gotta feed Toby.' Pop stops mid-stride. 'Go round up some wood.'

'For the stove?' I ask.

'For the barbie.'

'Right!' I gather up twigs and lumps of tree.

'Shove a couple of spuds under the coals when the fire dies down,' calls Pop.

'Where's the peeler?'

'A bit of dirt adds flavour.'

———

Sitting on a verandah and dipping sausage and spud in tomato sauce and swishing flies is awesome. And when Pop starts mashing his spuds I reckon I've learned more in the last five minutes than in the whole hundred million days at school.

After, Pop flicks his plate under the tap, then I do, and that's washing up. Night's creeping in when Pop says, 'Want to see something?' He strides off up a track, and I quickly follow. We turn down one after another until he stops. 'Look up!' he says.

'Wow!'

In the country the stars are bright and shiny. There are a million trillion of them hanging low like a curtain.

Back at the homestead, Pop says, 'Time to hit the hay, mister. It's up with the birds!'

In the little back bedroom it's dark like black with strange sounds that sneak in through the window. I stick my head under the blankets, close my ears and concentrate on sausages and mash.

I beat the birds to it, and by eight we're bumping over paddocks. There are lambs everywhere – bouncing about like little white balls with waggly tails and ears like aeroplane wings.

'You can open the gates, mister.'

I heave open a gate for Pop to drive through. Then I see something. 'That baby's lost!' I take off after it.

'Stop!' bellows Pop.

'It's lost its mum!'

'She'll come back to it, but if she smells your human smell on it, she won't

and it'll die. Every ewe knows her baby
by its sound and smell,' explains Pop.
'See, here she comes.'

'Oh. That is so cool.'

As the day goes on, we check fences
and dams and lambs till it's time for me
to gather up twigs and sticks for the
wood stove. As I start, I hear Pop
hurrying along the verandah.

'I've got a present for you,' he pants.
In his coat pocket is the tiniest baby
lamb. 'He's only a day old.'

'But you said you can't touch them.'

'His mum died. Quick, wrap him up
while I light the fire.'

I grab an old towel and pack him up
like a parcel. Then Pop puts him by the
fire, in a box filled with straw.

'Will he die?' I ask Pop.

'That's up to you, mister.'

'Me?'

Pop shows me how to feed the baby warm milk with sugar from a spoon, how to push open the tiny mouth to get it in.

'Please don't die, little lamb . . .' I whisper.

———

In the night I creep through the dark and into the kitchen to feed the baby sweet milk.

The next day he starts to drink from a bottle. The next he gollops down half the bottle.

'He'll live now,' says Pop. 'Thanks to you.'

I smile down at the baby. 'You're a clever Little Lambchops.'

By the weekend he's staggering up and falling over, then he's up again and headbutting me. If you don't know already, that is lamb speak for 'More milk!'

Next, he susses out the kitchen. He poops and pees all over the place – under chairs, tables and behind doors, which means a lot of scrubbing up for me. He follows me everywhere.

'I think he thinks I'm his mum!' I tell Pop.

'That means you've done well, mister.' There's a pause while Pop scratches his head – or, rather, his hat. 'For a ten-year-old you're bit of a hero round here.'

I laugh. 'But, Pop, I'm eight and a half!'

'Well, I'll be a rabbit's uncle.' Pop turns to the lamb that is pooping on a letter that's blown onto the floor. 'As for you, the quicker you're out in the paddock with the others the better.'

'Baa baa baa,' goes Little Lambchops.

Pop tells me tomorrow is my last day on the farm. I can hardly believe it, but it proves one thing – time flies when you're having fun.

That night we have a barbie with sausages and spuds baked in the coals. When it gets dark we watch the stars, and it's like I'm inside a storybook with pictures.

'I have to go Little Lambchops,' I say. 'But I'll be back – promise.'

'He'll always belong to you, mister,' says Pop.

Suddenly, I have an idea. 'Can I put one of those tag things on him so I can spot him when I come back?'

Pop nods. 'We'll put a green marker in his ear.'

'Then, Little Lambchops, you really will be mine,' I say.

'Baa, baa, baa,' goes Little Lambchops.

———

A whole season passes before the car races once more towards the farm.

I try to read my book but all the time I'm thinking about my little lamb. I close my eyes and see four matchstick legs, two aeroplane ears and a little pink tongue slurping milk.

We arrive to find that Pop has left us a note on the kitchen table. He is at the cattle sales. So Dad gets busy chopping wood and Mum gets busy putting the kettle on, and I shoot off, yelling, 'I'm back, Little Lambchops!'

I charge up tracks to where sheep graze. I climb fences, going from one paddock to the next. Fat woolly sheep look up and run as I come near.

The sun is setting as Pop's Land Rover comes winding along the drive but still I walk and walk.

'Where are you, Little Lambchops?'

There's no strong fat lamb with an ear tag anywhere . . .

The only green marker I can see is on the ear of a very large, very woolly sheep that is standing on its own with its head down, grazing on the thick grass.

SCARY FAIRIES

BY DAVID HARDING

Ned was a boy, everyone could tell.

His favourite colour was blue, he loved getting dirty and he always watched the wrestling on TV. Ned ran around the backyard, rode a skateboard and played video games.

His sister Charlotte was different. She was a girl, everyone could tell.

Her bedsheets were pink, all of her clothes were pink, and her favourite drink was strawberry milk. Most of all, Charlotte loved fairies. She had pictures of fairies all over her bedroom.

One Saturday morning, Ned was very bored. There was nothing exciting on TV and he had finished all of his video games. He walked into Charlotte's room to see what she was doing. His dog Spike followed him.

Charlotte was prancing around her room in her ballet dress. She wore a tiara in her curly, brown hair, and two pink fairy wings were strapped to her back.

'I am the fairy princess,' she said.

'Yuck!' said Ned. 'I don't like fairies.'

'I love them,' said Charlotte.

'You know, they aren't even real,' said Ned.

'Yes, they are,' said Charlotte. 'They are beautiful – and magic.'

Ned groaned. 'Come on, Spike,' he said, 'let's go and play out the back.'

Spike raced to the back door of the
house and barked. Ned opened the door
and they both ran into the backyard.
Ned and Spike chased each other
around. Then they played fetch with
a frisbee.

When he had had enough, Ned sat
down to rest under the big tree that
grew in the back corner of the backyard.
Spike flopped down in the shade next to
him. Ned gazed up at the house and saw
Charlotte's bedroom window. It was open
and he could hear her singing a song
about fairies. Then she twirled past the
window.

Ned threw away his frisbee in disgust.
'Gross,' he said. 'You think fairies are
dumb too, don't you, Spike?'

Spike laid his head in Ned's lap and closed his eyes.

'Yeah, fairies are so stupid,' said Ned.

Just then, Ned's frisbee flew back through the air and hit him on the forehead.

'Ow!' he said, rubbing his head. 'How did that happen?'

'I threw it,' said a voice. It was an angry voice that sounded like feet walking on gravel.

'Who's there?' asked Ned.

'I won't come out until you say sorry

for calling fairies stupid and dumb,' said the voice.

Spike sniffed. Ned did too. A terrible smell was wafting through the air.

'Um, okay,' Ned said to the invisible voice with the strong smell. 'I'm sorry. I shouldn't have said fairies were dumb.'

'Well, that's better,' said the voice.

Then, with a sound like tearing paper, the owner of the voice appeared – a tiny man floating in the air! He had dirty green clothes, messy hair and four small wings that fluttered at a million miles a minute.

'My name is Grumbles, and I am a fairy,' he said. Grumbles zipped back and forth in front of Ned's face. 'Don't you ever call fairies rude names again!'

'No, I won't,' said Ned, covering his nose. Grumbles smelled like mud mixed with dead leaves.

Spike began jumping around to nip Grumbles, but the fairy flew too fast to be caught.

'Please tell your dog to stop,' said Grumbles, 'or I will use my angry magic.'

Ned held on to Spike and stared at Grumbles. He thought fairies were supposed to be pretty and wear pink and purple. Grumbles was messy and liked to throw frisbees at people's heads.

'How many fairies are there?' asked Ned.

'Lots,' said Grumbles. 'Would you like to see?'

Ned wasn't sure. 'Are they all like you?' he asked.

'You'll see,' said Grumbles. 'First, I need to say the magic words.' He spat on the ground. Ned had to jump out of the way.

'I didn't realise that fairies are so disgusting,' said Ned.

Grumbles spun around on his spit and lightning crackled out of his fingers as he sang:

Yucky, mucky, scrunchy, scary.
Welcome to the world of fairies!

All of a sudden, Grumbles, Ned and Spike were in a different place. It was stinky, muddy, messy and full of fairies. Each fairy was dirty and smelly too. None of them said hello, but rudely turned away from Ned when they saw him. One or two were picking their

tiny noses as green snot bubbled out
of them.

'Welcome to Fairy Land,' said
Grumbles, 'the worst place in the world.'

'It's terrible,' said Ned. 'Why do you
live here?'

'Because we like it,' snapped an old
fairy, flying past with mud in his beard.
'And it's none of your business, anyway.'

'A fairy's favourite thing is to make
people cranky,' said Grumbles. 'Here,
we hide and make our awful plans.'

'What plans?' asked Ned, covering his
nose again. Grumbles' breath smelled
like old tuna.

'Have you ever tripped over
something? Or lost your favourite
pencil?' asked Grumbles. 'People think

that's all just bad luck. But they are wrong. That's when a fairy is being mean to you!'

By now, dozens of dirty fairies were flying around Ned and Grumbles. They were covered in yellow, snotty slime and looking at Ned like they wanted to push him over. Spike yapped at them.

'But why do fairies like being cruel?' asked Ned.

'FOR FUN!' shouted all the fairies. And then they sang:

It's fun to be so rude and scary,

Watch out world, here come the fairies!

'No one can see us,' said Grumbles, 'so no one can blame us. It's terribly funny!'

Ned had had enough of these terrible creatures. He looked at his watch. 'Sorry,' he said, 'but my sister's dance recital is on this afternoon. I have to go home.'

The scary fairies winked at each other. Some started to chuckle.

Grumbles sent Ned and Spike home again with his magic. Ned ran inside with Spike and slammed the door. 'I hope I never meet *them* again,' he said.

Ned walked into the living room. His mum was packing Charlotte's dancing bag. 'Are you ready to go, Ned?' she asked.

'Yes,' he said, 'let's go right away.'

Charlotte bounced in, wearing a pink tutu and her fairy wings. 'Don't you think I look like a fairy?' she asked.

'Not really,' said Ned. 'Fairies don't look like that at all.'

Charlotte stamped her foot and turned away. 'You don't know anything,' she said.

They all got into the car and drove to the dance studio. There, Ned and his mum left Charlotte backstage to get ready for the show. Lots of little girls in tutus and fairy wings ran about, giggling.

Ned and his mum sat in the front row, right near the stage. Huge curtains were pulled back to reveal the stage full of pink, cardboard scenery. A sign hanging from the curtain read 'Fairyland'.

Then Charlotte's dance teacher, Miss Rose, began to play a piano that was in the right corner of the stage. The performance was starting.

'Pssst!' said a voice.

Ned turned but couldn't see anyone. 'Who's there?'

'It's me, Grumbles,' whispered the invisible fairy. 'Thanks for telling us about this concert. We're all here. This is going to be fun!'

'No!' yelled Ned.

'*Shh!*' hissed his mum. 'Don't be so rude.'

Ned slunk down into his chair.

The first ballerinas skipped out onto the stage in a line. Suddenly, the front dancer tripped and fell. The dancer behind crashed on top of her, and then all the other girls in tutus did the same. Each ballerina ended up on the floor with their legs in the air.

All the parents stood up in horror. The dance teacher stopped playing. Only Ned could hear the fairies laughing their heads off.

Soon, everyone was back in their places to restart the concert. This time no one fell over.

'Phew,' said Ned.

Charlotte twirled onto stage. Ned's mum clapped. As she spun across the stage, Charlotte's tights ripped and the fairy wings on her back slipped off.

'Hey!' Ned shouted to the fairies. 'Stop that!'

Everyone in the audience told him to be quiet. Charlotte's face was red. She stamped her foot, fixed her wings and resumed her routine. Ned sat low in his chair. Then, one of the cardboard trees started to rock back and forth.

The fairies are going to tip it over! Ned thought to himself.

Just as Charlotte sprang towards the tree, Ned jumped up onto the stage.

'Ned, how dare you!' called his mum. 'Come back here this instant!'

Ned ignored his mum. He ran over to the tree and caught it before it could land on his sister.

Everyone watching was amazed. Then they clapped. The dance teacher came

over and asked if Ned and Charlotte
were all right. Ned nodded and put the
tree back into place.

Their mum climbed onto the stage
and gave Charlotte a hug. 'She's okay
thanks to you, Ned,' she said.

Ned listened for the tiny laughter, but
he couldn't hear it anymore. Perhaps
he had spoiled the scary fairies' fun and
they had left.

After the performance, Ned and his
family walked back to their car. On the
way, Ned heard a very loud burp coming
from the bushes on his right. He turned
and saw a dirty white horse wearing an
eye patch. The horse also had a long,
white horn protruding from its forehead.

The unicorn burped again. 'If you

think fairies are bad, you should see what
unicorns are like!' it said.

Ned screamed and ran all the way to
the car. He jumped inside and slammed
the door behind him.

His mother and
sister both shook
their heads and
rolled their eyes.
They didn't
understand boys
at all.

THE GOBLIN PRINCESS

BY FIONA MCDONALD

Aubergine was the daughter of the King of the Goblins. She lived in a glittering palace deep within the earth. Her bedroom was made of crystal, her bed was carved from gold, rubies dotted the ceiling and her diamond window looked out upon a garden of jewels.

Aubergine was very beautiful, too. She had large bulbous eyes, a tiny turned-up nose and her green, mossy hair fell in heavy locks past her shoulders and almost to her shapely feet with their one delicate toe.

A goblin princess works hard. She must know all the laws of her country so she can rule wisely and kindly. She must learn the names of all the gemstones, minerals and metals that are found in the ground, as well as the little animals that live amongst them.

Aubergine had lessons every morning. But every afternoon, when the whole goblin kingdom took a well-earned nap, Aubergine would slip out of her window, into her sparkly garden and into the caves and tunnels to explore.

One day Aubergine wandered far from home. She had seen all there was to see of her own kingdom and longed to find something mysterious and exciting.

'I shall have to turn back soon,' she said to herself as she trotted up a steep set of stairs. Their ancient surface was worn with the years of many feet walking up and down them. Moss made them slippery, and a couple of times Aubergine fell and grazed her knees.

A light grew steadily brighter as she neared the mouth of the cave. Suddenly, Aubergine stood looking down on the most amazing sight she'd ever seen.

Spread out below her was a landscape such as she'd only seen in books of fairytales. Everything was green, not

emerald green but softer. Tall objects
stood up in groups here and there,
though some stood alone.

'Trees!' guessed Aubergine. 'This
must be the upper world. I do hope
I don't blow off into the sky and become
lost forever.'

Hesitantly, Aubergine took a step
out of the cave and into that delicious,
beckoning greenness. Strange smells
wafted to her. She inhaled deeply and
spluttered as they hit the back of her
throat.

What was that ribbon of silver in the
distance? Aubergine ran down the slope
and found herself beside a river. A river
in the upper world? It was so different to
the slow-moving, clear and cold waters

of her home. This water chuckled and giggled as it rollicked away. Green weed, not unlike her own hair, waved under the surface.

Aubergine stuck a foot in the river and shrieked with its tickling. Something swooped out of the air and flicked past her nose. What could it be, this thing that twittered?

'Birds, I expect,' said Aubergine. 'Just like in the books at home.'

On she wandered under the brilliant blue sky. She'd forgotten she needed to get home. Everything was so glorious and exciting.

'A village!'

Aubergine ran towards the cluster of little houses with thatched roofs and pretty gardens. She stuck her tiny nose into the heads of enormous roses and nearly fainted from their perfume. The colours danced before her and she thought she'd die with the joy of it all.

'What do you think you're doing?' said an angry voice that made her jump. 'Get away, you ugly creature. Be gone, go back to your infernal hole!'

Aubergine wasn't sure she understood at first, but the look on the old woman's face soon enlightened her. She mumbled an apology and fled.

Soon, she came upon children playing in the street, jumping rope and singing. Aubergine knew this game and the song that went with it. She ran into

their midst and began jumping and
singing with them.

'Ah, it's a goblin!' shrieked one of the
children. 'Run!'

The children scattered, racing
towards the safety of their homes.

Aubergine stood there, bewildered.
What were they scared of? 'I only want
to play,' she said in a small voice. She
picked up the rope and gave it a couple
of turns but she didn't want to jump on
her own.

With her head down, and tears rolling down her cheeks, Aubergine walked along the road until she left the village behind her. The sun beat on the back of her neck and gave her a headache. She wanted to go home.

But where was home?

She looked around and found she could no longer see the mountains. The village had disappeared, too. Tall buildings loomed over her and she crouched in their cold shadows. This was not a nice place. There were nasty smells and black rats ran over heaps of rotting rubbish. Aubergine had never heard of a place like this before and she was afraid. Creeping along the walls, watching where she put her feet, Aubergine made her way through the darkness that was night, wishing she had not strayed so far from home.

'Where are you going?' A hand gripped her shoulder; Aubergine turned and looked up into the face of a tall man. He had a scar down one side of his face and his smile was twisted with cruelty.

Aubergine tried to run but she was held tight.

'I think I know just the place for you, my lovely,' the man whispered in her ear. Aubergine could smell his onion breath. She felt the danger in his long fingers sinking into her very bones and seeping downwards to her heart. Before she could flee, the man's other hand grabbed her round the waist and hauled her off into the night.

The cage door shut with a clang. Aubergine flung herself onto the dirty straw and wept.

Day after day, long travelling days of jolting and jerking as the cage was pulled by a weary old horse, Aubergine grew grey and quiet. Her hair lost its green lustre and began to look like the straw on which she slept. Tears stained her dirty face and she grew thinner and thinner.

In the evenings the tents were put up, the lights were set and the crowds came. They glared and jeered at her through the bars. Sometimes they threw scraps of food, sometimes nasty things like rotten eggs. Children screamed when they caught sight of her and women fainted. Aubergine crept as far from them as she could, hid her face in her arms and longed for her mountain home.

She would let her mind wander down corridors of smooth, cool rock. She would go up and down the stone steps and across the deep, still underground pools but nowhere even in her deepest memory could she find her home.

'This one's lost its appeal.' The show master approached Aubergine's cage and poked her with a stick. 'It's looking sick. We ain't got room for unhealthy, unhappy exhibits. Get rid of it.'

Before she knew what was happening, Aubergine's door was flung open. Rough hands dragged her out and threw her onto the ground. She lay in the dust until the wagons and carts dwindled into minute specks on the road.

Slowly, Aubergine got to her feet and stretched up as far as she could. It had been so long since she'd been able to stand. She looked at her thin arms and the scabs on her skinny legs. As her fingers felt the dry, flaky skin on her face, she smiled. She was free. She could finally go home.

Aubergine travelled at night, stealing food from farmhouses along the way. She ate raw eggs and pulled carrots from gardens. Dogs barked at her, but she soon grew adept at hiding and fading into the night.

And when she curled up to sleep under a tree root, or deep in the straw of a barn, she would murmur, 'I'm going home.' Aubergine would fall asleep with a smile on her face because she knew she would get there one day. And she did.

CHARLIE AND LOU THE SHARK

BY GRACE ATWOOD

The aquarium in Charlie's home town had been designed and built in the shape of a shark. The shark's mouth was the entrance to the building and you had to walk in past rows and rows of sharp, pointy teeth. This meant that very few little girls wanted to visit the aquarium because, as everyone knows, little girls do not like sharks.

Every day at about ten in the morning you would see well-meaning mums and dads trying to pull their fearful daughters towards the entrance of the aquarium. There would be tantrum-throwing, howling and screaming. Most parents would give up in frustration, cursing the architect and the city council for being so hopeless when it came to designing buildings little girls would want to enter.

The Clown Fish ice-cream parlour next to the aquarium did a roaring trade because, as everyone knows, the only way to quieten down a hysterical little girl is to buy her a double scoop of boysenberry swirl ice-cream. It's all very well to cut

up carrot sticks for a healthy snack,
but they will be no good whatsoever
when you're confronted with a building
that resembles a shark.

Charlie had a boy's name but she
was a girl. And Charlie had never been
afraid of the aquarium. In fact, it was her
favourite place to go on sunny days,
on windy days and on rainy days. Her poor
nanny, a very nice lady called Poppy
Lock, could not convince Charlie to visit
anywhere else. This was terrible news for
Poppy because she had a paralysing fear
of water.

Every day at a quarter past ten,
after they'd walked through the rows
of sharp pointy teeth to get inside the
aquarium, Charlie would sit Poppy at

the cafe, facing away from the massive fish tank with the piranhas in it, and would organise a soothing hot chocolate to calm her nanny's nerves. If Charlie hadn't been such a sweetie, Poppy Lock would have found another little girl to look after. But, apart from her love of aquariums, Poppy thought Charlie was the most almost-perfect little girl in the world.

Once Charlie had settled her nanny and made sure she had a book with no references to water in it to read, Charlie would grab her shark hat from her backpack, pull it carefully over her pigtails and go in search of Lou.

Lou was an ugly 16-year-old hammerhead shark, covered in barnacles and scratches from years of in-tank brawling. If a shark had been able to get a tattoo, Charlie knew Lou would have demanded a pirate's skull and crossbones inked onto his dorsal fin.

The visitors wandering around the aquarium appreciating the dainty sea dragons and the graceful manta rays would always point at Lou with a shudder.

'What a terrifying shark!'

'He'd eat me in a flash if I was in the tank with him.'

'Doesn't he have a lopsided hammer?'

All of those statements were true, but that just made Charlie love him more.

And Lou felt the same way about Charlie. The double glazing of the aquarium tank didn't stop Lou from seeing the horrified looks of the visitors as he swam past, looking ferocious. He'd become used to it over the years and had worked on perfecting a toothy sneer and a snappy tail whip. But he remembered the first day he noticed the little girl with the shark hat staring through the glass at him. Instead of distaste or fear, Charlie looked at him affectionately. Her expression didn't even change after he performed his nasty tail whip.

After her third visit to the aquarium, Lou the shark swam over to the thick glass separating the sea creatures from the visitors, not bothering with his fearsome tail whip. He stared at her closely. Because a hammerhead has an eye on each end

of its wide head, he
could only stare at her
with one eye at a time.
Charlie didn't mind.
She stayed still, as calm
as a sea cucumber,
staring back at him
with a huge grin on
her face.

When Lou realised that Charlie was
not scared of him in the slightest, he
started to look forward to her visits.
He'd keep an eye out for the distinctive
shark hat (it wasn't a hammerhead that
adorned the hat, unfortunately. It was
one of those show-pony great whites
instead) and glide right up to the edge
of the glass and stare at her.

When one of the aquarium staff, who cleaned the inside of the aquarium tank, found a hammerhead shark tooth, she knew just who to give it to.

Charlie's mum drilled a tiny hole into the base of it and threaded a chain through it, and Charlie showed her new necklace to Lou next time she visited. He seemed thrilled. And so did the local press. There were articles, photos, shark information evenings, blog posts and tweets. The aquarium even splashed out and hired a sky writer to write:

Visit Lou the Shark at the Aquarium!

All of a sudden, the little girls in Charlie's home town realised they wanted to meet the famous Lou too, and there were no more tantrums outside the aquarium. Scores of little girls hopped and skipped over the teeth at the entrance without a second thought, elbowing little boys out of their way in their zeal to get to the shark tank.

The owner of the aquarium was so thrilled by the rise in visitor numbers that she gave Charlie a lifetime free pass to the aquarium. Charlie was grateful. She knew there were many other amazing sea creatures she could visit – moon jellys, fairy penguins and even green sea turtles – but she only had eyes for her best friend Lou: the biggest, ugliest and most famous hammerhead shark in the world.

THE DOG ATE MY HOMEWORK

BY GEORGE IVANOFF

THE EXCUSE

'The dog ate it,' mumbled Christopher.

'What?' asked Ms Simone, staring at her student.

'The dog ate my homework,' said Christopher, in a louder voice.

There were a few giggles from some of the other kids in the class. Ms Simone looked around sternly, and the class fell silent. 'That's not a very original excuse,' she said.

'But –' began Christopher.

'No buts,' said Ms Simone, cutting him off. 'This is the second time you haven't handed in your homework. Do you want me to send another note to your parents? I don't want to hear any more made-up excuses. I want the truth.'

'But it *is* true,' said Christopher. 'The dog ate my homework because of my PlayStation, the mud-pile, the gravy and the people chained to the tree.'

Ms Simone stared at him.

'Okay,' said Christopher, 'I'll start at the beginning . . .'

DOING HOMEWORK

I started my homework as soon as I got home from school. I know that's a bit weird, but there's a reason I did.

I usually play my PlayStation when I get home from school, but I can't at the moment because Mum and Dad put it away for a whole week. That's my punishment for not doing my homework last week. A whole *week* – I don't think that's fair.

Anyway, I couldn't play my PlayStation, and I couldn't play outside because our backyard is this huge pile of mud at the moment. It's true!

You see, Mum and Dad wanted to put a pool in for summer, and Dad decided he could do it himself. Mum wasn't happy about it, but he started digging up the backyard. He did a bit each day after work. But then we started to get all

that rain, and our whole backyard just turned to mud. If it gets any wetter we'll have a mudslide in the back room. Honest! The mud is almost right up against the back door.

Anyway, I couldn't play my PlayStation and I couldn't play in the backyard. I couldn't go to the park, either. See, the park is full of people chained to a huge tree. Honest!

The council was going to cut down some of the trees in the park because a branch fell on the Mayor. It was just a little branch . . . but it fell on his head, and then he fell over . . . right into the duck pond. So he wanted all the trees cut down.

But the Local Conversation Society decided to stop him. I mean, the Local Conservation Society. They say that the really big tree in the middle of the park is very old and shouldn't be cut down. So they chained themselves to it to stop it from being cut down. Then other people started to chain themselves to other trees. So now the park is full of people chained to trees, and reporters and people coming to watch the chained people. So there's no room to play.

Anyway, I couldn't play the PlayStation and I couldn't play in the backyard and I couldn't go to the park. So I did my homework instead. Honest!

UNCLE ANDREW, HENRY AND THE GRAVY

I finished my homework before dinner and put it on the coffee table in the lounge room. Then I went to set the table for dinner because on Mondays it's my turn to set the table.

Then my Uncle Andrew arrived because he sometimes comes over to have dinner with us. While we were having dinner, I told him about my homework. He asked if he could read it. Honest! He said he was interested.

So I went and got it for him right then and there. And he read it at the dinner table while eating his roast. But then he spilled some gravy on it. He tried to wipe it off with his napkin, but all he did was kind of smear the gravy all over it. Then he gave it back to me.

So I had gravy-smeared homework. I thought I'd copy it out after dinner, so I put it back on the coffee table while we had dessert.

Anyway, remember I said the backyard was just mud? So Henry is now living inside. Henry – that's my dog. He's one of those little sausage dogs. I think they're called duckhounds or something.

Anyway, Henry was in the lounge room and he must have smelled the

gravy on my homework. He loves gravy.
It's his favourite food, after sauerkraut –
that's this pickled cabbage stuff my
dad makes. I think it's yuck, but Henry
loves it.

Anyway, while we were all in the
dining room having our dessert, Henry
was in the lounge room eating my
gravy-smeared homework.

I wasn't happy when I found out what
he'd done. It meant I was going to have
to do my homework again.
But then Henry got a
tummy-ache from eating my
homework and we had
to rush him to the vet.
The vet's a friend
of my dad's. He wasn't

happy when we came over. Not because my homework got eaten, but because he was having his dinner when we showed up.

Henry had to spend the night there, but he's okay and he's coming home later today.

THE PRINCIPAL

'Well,' said the teacher, as the rest of the class laughed. 'That's certainly an interesting story. Now, I know that your homework was to write a creative essay, and your little excuse was certainly creative, but –'

Just at that moment there was a knock at the door.

'Excuse me, Ms Simone,' said the Principal as she entered the room.

'I've just had the strangest phone call.'

Ms Simone stared at the Principal.

'I have a message for Christopher Smit.' She turned to look around the room.

Christopher raised his hand. 'I'm Christopher Smit,' he said.

'I've got a message for you from your mother,' said the Principal. 'She says that she's caught in a traffic jam. Some protesters who were chained to a tree are now blocking traffic instead. And that your father is trying to stop a mudslide in your backyard. So she needs you to pick up Henry from the vet on your way home from school.'

Christopher looked at Ms Simone and smiled.

THE DOLLS' FIRST CHRISTMAS

BY SOPHIE MASSON

It was early on Christmas Eve, and the last delivery had just arrived at Miss Jeffries' toyshop. There were teddy bears and tin toys, puppets and pull-alongs, rocking horses and dolls' houses. And then there was Esmeralda.

Esmeralda had arrived in an ordinary box, just like Sarah, Donna, Laura, Clara and Gloria.

Gloria, the haughty queen of the dolls in Miss Jeffries' toyshop, sat on

her glittering throne in the window.
Everyone had gasped when they had first
seen Gloria and how beautiful she was.
But no one had bought her. She was *too*
special and cost too much.

Esmeralda was also beautiful, but in
a different way. Her hair wasn't golden,
like Gloria's, but black, in great long
curls. Her skin wasn't peaches and
cream, like Gloria's, but honey and tea.
Her eyes weren't sky blue, but hazel.
Her stripy dress was splendid, but she
did not have elegant satin slippers, like
Gloria. Her feet were bare.

Miss Jeffries smiled as she set
Esmeralda up on the green velvet
window display. 'There, now,' she said.
'We'll have two queens. A snow queen

and a sun queen. You'll be friends.'

But can two queens really be friends?
Gloria didn't think so. Esmeralda didn't
think so, either. Each doll thought she
was better than the other. Each sat in
her splendour and looked haughtily
away, thinking she would be the first
to go.

It was a long, busy day. Sarah and
Clara and Laura and Donna left, as did
two boy dolls, six tin toys, eight teddy
bears, three puppets, two fairy dolls,

a mermaid doll, two clowns, four baby dolls and a brace of Barbies. But not Gloria. And not Esmeralda, either.

At last, when Miss Jeffries was about to close the shop, a man rushed in.

'My boss, Mr Darling, has sent me to buy a Christmas gift for his daughter, Cherie,' the man shouted. 'Her mother has passed away and her father has no time to shop. I need your very best doll.'

'We have two of the very best dolls you will ever see,' said Miss Jeffries, calmly. 'Esmeralda and Gloria. Which one would Cherie like best? The sun queen or the snow queen?'

The man stared at the dolls. 'Oh! I have no idea, but I know Cherie will have a tantrum if she doesn't like what

I choose. She's always having tantrums.
Blow it, I'll take the two.'

Miss Jeffries beamed. 'Good choice!
They belong together, no question.'

She put them in their boxes and tied
a pretty ribbon around them, then waved
a cheerful goodbye as the man hurried
out.

'If that brat doesn't like one of them,
she can always give the doll to someone
else,' he muttered. 'Or throw it away.
They're only dolls, after all.'

Poor Gloria and Esmeralda! They had
been made with such care. Their dresses
were hand-stitched, their hair delicately
plaited by hand, their faces handpainted.
They'd been made to be loved. And now
here was someone saying they might

just be thrown away, like some cheap factory toy.

Dolls may not talk, and their red satin hearts may not beat, but they have other ways of communicating. Gloria and Esmeralda sensed each other's fear.

Most dolls are airheads, the space under their pretty china or plastic skulls quite hollow. But Gloria and Esmeralda had cloth faces, pulled tightly over wads of stuffing. In the middle of the stuffing, each had a long, bright pin, left in by mistake. So their thoughts were sharp, and they each thought the same thing at the same moment. They were queens! They might not be friends, but sometimes queens put rivalry aside

for the good of all. They would do
something together, not apart. But what?

———

At the Darling mansion, the man handed
over the boxes to the housekeeper.
She took them to a room where a tall,
twinkling Christmas tree stood. Piles of
presents were stacked underneath it.

The housekeeper shook her head
sadly. 'More things going to waste on that
spoilt child,' she said.

The dolls lay under the tree for
hours, but no clever ideas came to them.
Soon, they knew, it would be too late.

Just after midnight, they heard the
clatter of hooves on the roof. Moments
later, a deep voice grumbled, 'Why do
I come? She has so much already!'

All toys, no matter how new they
are, know what happens on Christmas
night. So Esmeralda and Gloria knew
the grumbler wasn't Mr Darling or any
of his staff. It was that jolly visitor, come
from a magical world, whose job is to
give every child in the world a present.
The humans call him Santa Claus.

The dolls' red satin hearts swelled
and the sharp pin in their heads glittered
as they tried to struggle out to beg for his
help. They only managed a tiny rustle,
but Santa Claus' sharp ears pricked up.

And his kind eyes, which can see into the heart of every child, saw right into theirs. With a little chuckle, he opened the boxes. He gazed in at Esmeralda and Gloria.

'A Christmas gift for you, little ones?' he said. He touched each of them very gently. A warm, golden stream of light seemed to flow from his fingers and into the dolls' painted eyes. 'Very well, then. I give you the power of love. And a very merry Christmas to you both.'

And with that, he was gone. The dolls heard the clatter of his reindeers' hooves on the roof, then nothing. They waited in the warm darkness, now filled with hope.

———

The next morning the dolls heard a man's voice.

'Well, Cherie, aren't you going to open your lovely presents?' he said, trying to sound jolly. 'Start with those two boxes.'

'Yes, Daddy,' said a thin, flat voice.

Gloria and Esmeralda were afraid again. This child would *not* love them, no matter what Santa Claus said. All was lost.

Next thing, the wrapping paper was roughly ripped, the lids of the boxes pulled off so quickly that the dolls fell out and onto their faces.

'Really, Cherie, be careful!' cried Mr Darling. 'Look how beautiful they are!'

'I don't like dolls,' shouted Cherie. 'They stare and stare and they're stupid!'

'Oh, nothing's good enough for you! I'm tired of it. Tired, do you hear?' yelled her father. He left the room, slamming the door behind him.

Cherie glared at the dolls. She picked them up roughly. Gloria and Esmeralda thought their last hour had come. They would be torn limb from limb, their bodies shredded, their heads wrenched off.

But as they helplessly looked up, they saw a sadness in the child's eyes that made their red satin hearts clench and their sharp minds ache. In that instant, something warm and golden and loving flowed from the dolls to the child, seeping into Cherie's unhappy, lonely eyes.

She stared at them. Her bottom lip trembled. 'I don't like dolls,' she said faintly. Shyly, she touched Esmeralda's hair, then Gloria's. She stroked their clothes. She held a doll in the crook of each arm. 'Most dolls are stupid,' she whispered. 'But not you.'

That is how Mr Darling found them when he came back, ashamed of shouting at his daughter on Christmas Day, telling himself that he must be more patient, even if she made it hard.

Cherie smiled at him. 'Daddy,' she said. 'Do you know what their names are? Gloria and Esmeralda. I think they must be good friends, don't you? Oh, Daddy, I love them already.'

As Mr Darling sat with his daughter,

Gloria and Esmeralda lay happily in her arms. Can two queens really be good friends? Why not? Anything was possible on this beautiful Christmas morning.

MALVOLIO, MRS TOSCA AND BOZO THE DOG

BY VASHTI FARRER

Malvolio the duck had feathers as scruffy as an old coat. His tail stuck out behind him like a rolled-up newspaper. His chest was spotted as if he'd spilt crumbs down his shirt front, and the skin around his beak and eyes was all wrinkly and red.

Malvolio was *not* a handsome duck by any means, but he made up for it by being bold and fearless. Malvolio wasn't

afraid of anything,
except perhaps of
Mrs Tosca's dog, Bozo.

Bozo was big and
brown and shaggy.
His pointy ears stuck
straight up and he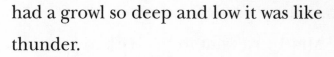
had a growl so deep and low it was like
thunder.

All the water birds knew to keep well
away from Bozo. That is, all except for
Malvolio. He wasn't scared because he
thought he was *smarter* than Bozo any
day. But twice, quite recently, Malvolio
had barely escaped when Bozo had
chased him. He'd had to swim like mad
to get back to the bird island in the
middle of the lake. He'd finished up with

a very sore tail and Bozo had been left with a mouthful of tail feathers.

Every day, old Mrs Tosca took Bozo to the park for walkies. Now, secretly, Mrs Tosca was scared of birds. She'd hoped that, by feeding the ducks and other birds, she'd get used to them. She took Bozo along partly for protection.

Mrs Tosca went to the park to practise her singing. She had once been an opera singer, so she could sing very well. But every time she tried to sing in her flat, her neighbours would complain that they couldn't concentrate.

'QUIET!' they'd yell from upstairs, banging their floor with a shoe. 'We're trying to work!'

'Philistines!' Mrs Tosca would shout

back. Then she'd rattle Bozo's lead and he'd wake up and wag his tail, knowing that it meant one thing – walkies!

Now, Mrs Tosca had very fine, white hair that was just perfect for lining nests. So whenever she and Bozo went walking in the park, the birds would swoop down and help themselves to bits of her hair.

Mrs Tosca would shriek when this happened, and when Mrs Tosca shrieked, Bozo would growl and start barking at the birds. But that only made Mrs Tosca cross with Bozo for frightening the birds, and she would hurry home, her hair sticking up like ruffled feathers.

For Bozo, the worst part of going to the park was when Mrs Tosca stopped to feed the ducks. He didn't want to stop.

He wanted to check on his tree-mails. There were always interesting messages left on trees, such as:

Rover, fun-loving red setter, has run away from home. Needs new digs.

Fifi, French poodle, looking for romance. Please leave message, darling. xxx

Scruffy. Mutt. Down on his luck, looking to share kennel and fleas. Sam.

But Bozo never had time to finish checking his messages, because he always had to take care of Mrs Tosca when she went to feed the water birds. Once they reached the lake, Mrs Tosca would tie

Bozo to a metal pole and say, 'Sit!' Then she'd sing to the ducks, pretending they were a real, live audience and she was standing on a proper stage.

Some days she would sing:

Quack, quack, quack! Quacky ducks!
Quack, quack, quack! Quacky ducks!

On other days, she might sing:

Near the lake you'll find me!
Opening up my bread bag!

And, of course, the ducks and water birds would come paddling frantically towards her. Mrs Tosca tried hard not to be nervous, but she was always

worried the birds might start plucking
at her hair.

'What if they take all of it for their
nests?' she'd say. 'I'll end up bald!'
But rather than let them *see* she was
scared, she would sing:

I have the crumbs, I have the bread!
I have the bread, I have the crumbs!
Swim across to me and I will fill your
little tums.

Now, of all the birds on the island,
Malvolio was the greediest. All day long,
he would watch people come to the lake,
hoping they were there just to feed him.
And as soon as he heard the crackle of
a bread bag, he'd be off, black legs and

yellow feet paddling like crazy across the water to make sure he reached the bank first. The other birds were never far behind, but they could never catch Malvolio.

And Malvolio always knew when Mrs Tosca was there. The sound of her paper bag crackled over the water while she sang and the wind blew her fine, white nesting hair around her face.

No sooner would Malvolio hear her singing, than he'd slip into the water and start swimming towards the bank. Up he would go, elbowing the other birds out of the way, with a 'Buzz off!' at the swans, a 'BOO!' at the little, black

moorhens and a 'SHOO!' to the noisy
seagulls.

One morning that seemed like any
other day, Mrs Tosca was surrounded by
birds and feeling especially nervous. But,
still, she tried to make sure they all had
enough to eat, even if Malvolio ended up
gobbling the most.

'More! More!' he quacked between
mouthfuls. 'ME! ME! ME! Get out of my
way, I was here first!'

The moorhens pecked up the crumbs
at her feet. The seagulls squealed and
swooped for crusts that had fallen on the
water. The swans stretched out their long
necks for bits that were left on the bank,
and, in the middle, almost standing on
Mrs Tosca's feet, was greedy Malvolio,
stuffing his beak.

Meanwhile, Bozo sat nearby, tied to his pole and watching. He didn't trust the birds not to attack Mrs Tosca. *Especially* that Malvolio.

Just then, the biggest of the black swans reached for a scrap of bread that Malvolio was planning to eat next.

'That's mine!' he quacked, his mouth full.

The swan tried to bite him, but Malvolio backed away with a squawk.

'*STOP IT!*' shrieked Mrs Tosca, throwing the bread in the air in fright.

'*GROOF! GROOF!*' barked Bozo, straining forward. He pulled and pulled until, suddenly, he uprooted the pole. Now free, he raced after Malvolio, dragging the pole behind him.

The little birds flew off in a fright.
The others plunged into the pond and
swam away.

'*HONK!*' went the swans, gliding off
in a huff.

Old Mrs Tosca tried to grab
Bozo's lead but missed. Bozo was
chasing Malvolio round and round the
park. Malvolio darted this way and that,
with Bozo scarcely a whisker behind him
and the pole clanking and bumping
along the ground.

Malvolio doubled back to the lake and dived in. The water was cool and green under the pink waterlilies, but Malvolio didn't notice. He swam faster than ever before, back to the safety of the island.

Across the water, Mrs Tosca was shouting, 'BAD BOZO!' as she grabbed his lead and marched him home. She was so cross her hair was sticking up like an upside-down nest.

When Malvolio reached the island his tail was quite bare. Never before had Bozo come so close. With more than half his tail feathers missing, Malvolio had to sit down *very* carefully.

He realised he'd had a really narrow escape and that maybe it was time to turn over a new leaf. From now on, he would keep as far away from Bozo as possible. Not only that, but he would try *not* to annoy the swans and other birds in case they upset Bozo. He resolved to no longer try to be first duck up the bank, but would wait till the others had set off before swimming after them. *And* he would only take his share of Mrs Tosca's bread.

It wasn't long before the other birds noticed the change in Malvolio. He was now a different duck altogether. Mrs Tosca noticed it too, and as time went by, she became less nervous around the snappy Malvolio. Best of all, even Bozo noticed. He still preferred collecting tree-mails to feeding the ducks, but at least he no longer felt he had to chase them. Now he simply sat beside his pole and listened to Mrs Tosca sing.

OVERCOMING AWESOME OGRE

BY GOLDIE ALEXANDER

Draggle and his family live in a cave on the summit of Fiery Mountain. Draggle's cousins are tops at everything dragons can do.

'One flick of my tail will cause an avalanche,' skites Fury.

'My breath will scorch the next mountain peak,' brags Ferocious.

'I've killed two princes and six knights,' Fiendish claims.

But Draggle is different. No matter how much he wants to be like his cousins, his tail drags in the dust, and when he tries to breathe fire, all that comes out is smoke. His cousins sneer and call him names like Bedraggled, Dusty, sometimes even Steam.

At the same time, every dragon is scared of the ogre who lives in the next valley.

'Awesome Ogre owns enough gold to reach our ceiling,' Great Uncle Ember growls.

Great Aunt Ember sprays fire and says, 'He can eat a man in one mouthful –'

'While it's said a dragon takes two,' Grandma Burn reminds her.

'The worst is,' Blaze roars, 'Awesome can change shape whenever he feels like it.'

'Don't worry about Awesome,' Grandpa Burn grumbles. 'Just look at Dragon Cave's roof and floor. We've breathed out so much fire everything's burnt and crumbling away.'

'Can't afford any repairs,' Uncle Fire says flatly. 'We've run out of gold.'

Grandpa Burn glares at the younger dragons. 'How come no one will tackle Awesome and bring home his treasure? In my time youngsters thought nothing of fighting ogres and giants . . .'

The cousins quake all over as they discuss ways and means of battling Awesome. But Draggle hides in the forest where no one will find him. He knows he can't fight anyone, much less someone this scary.

———

Not far from Fiery Mountain is Castle Bravery, where princes who fight dragons and ogres live. When these princes aren't fighting, they're jousting, fencing and polishing armour.

Arthur, the smallest prince, is different. He doesn't want to kill dragons or ogres. He's bad at jousting and fencing. He finds polishing armour boring.

Meanwhile, his mother, Princess Catalina, is very upset by the state of their castle. 'It needs fixing,' she says, pointing at their crumbling walls, burst water pipes, broken windows and rotten floorboards. 'Only, we haven't any gold to pay for repairs.'

Arthur would very much like to find enough gold to fix Castle Bravery, but he can't think how. Like Draggle, he's also called names – such as Cowardly, Gutless, even Gormless.

When this happens Arthur wanders deep into the forest, where he practices jousting and fencing. But what usually happens is that he trips over his lance, or his sword gets stuck in a tree.

———

One day, as Arthur is wandering through the forest, he feels something drip onto his head. He looks up to see a dragon crouched halfway up a tree. Tears are rolling down the dragon's face. Even though this dragon is no bigger than a boy, Arthur's heart gallops and he starts to run away.

'Please don't go,' the dragon calls after him. 'I won't hurt you.'

Arthur turns to ask, 'How do I know you won't?'

'Because I'm much too lonely,' says the dragon. More tears fall. 'Will you play with me?' He slithers down to the ground and holds out a paw. 'I'm Draggle.'

'I'm Arthur.' He holds out his hand. 'I've never been this close to a dragon.'

'I've never been this close to a boy,' says Draggle.

'Don't you breathe fire, steal treasure and scare people?' Arthur asks.

Draggle's tail droops in the dust. 'Not really,' he admits. 'All I can do is puff smoke. I don't much like fighting.'

Arthur settles on the ground beside Draggle. He likes the dragon's big eyes, alert ears and multicoloured coat. 'I don't much like fighting, either,' he confides. Then he adds, 'I like telling jokes.'

Draggle's laugh sounds like a washing machine with a crackly cog. 'Me too,' he says.

'What's your best joke?'

Draggle's tail thumps the ground. 'How do you calm a fire breathing dragon?'

'I know that one,' Arthur carols. 'Throw water at him and he'll let off steam. Here's another: Why do dragons sleep in the daytime?'

'So they can hunt *k*-nights,' Draggle yells.

They swap more jokes.

'How do you buy a wild duck? By really annoying a tame one.'

'Did you hear about the monster with five legs? They fitted him like a glove.'

They have such a good time they arrange to meet every day to tell more jokes.

———

Three weeks later the king's messenger turns up to Castle Bravery. He blows his

trumpet before announcing, 'Awesome
Ogre has eaten too many of the king's
subjects, so his majesty is offering a
reward for his capture.'

Everyone shudders. No one is brave
enough to even think of battling an ogre
as strong and big and scary as Awesome.

'Does he have any weakness?'
someone asks.

The messenger looks grim. 'It's said
that if you can make him laugh, he'll
shrivel into nothing.'

This gives Arthur an idea. He goes off to meet Draggle. 'What if our jokes can make Awesome laugh? He owns enough gold to fix Castle Bravery and Dragon Cave.'

Draggle is so scared, smoke comes out of his mouth and some birds flying overhead think a storm is coming. 'No one has ever survived Awesome,' he warns Arthur. 'You know what'll happen if he doesn't laugh.'

Though Arthur's heart is ready to jump out of his chest, he asks, 'Will you come with me?'

Draggle visibly gulps. But he can't let his new friend down. 'Only if you bring lots of sandwiches.'

Back home Arthur packs enough food to last one prince and one dragon several days. At the last minute, thinking it might get cold, he wears his warmest coat and returns to where Draggle is waiting.

———

They set off briskly. Crossing the next mountain range, they descend into a valley. Halfway across, they come to a river.

Draggle shivers as he looks at the strong current. 'Can't get through this,' he says, secretly relieved they can't go any further.

'No worries,' says Arthur, and he uses his sword to fell and cut a tree. Draggle helps him place the trunk between rocks.

They cross the river and walk through a dark forest, reaching the next mountain just as daylight is fading.

They're settling in for the night when an old man appears from behind a rock and hobbles towards them. Sighting Draggle and Arthur, he says angrily, 'Don't you know this mountain belongs to me? Unless I'm given three presents, I won't let you pass.'

To their dismay, he grows and grows. Soon, he is towering well above them and they realise they've walked straight into Awesome Ogre.

His head is as big as Bravery Castle, his mouth as wide as their biggest chimney, and his body as large as Dragon Cave. His legs are like enormous tree trunks. He's their worst nightmare come to life.

Though Arthur's teeth chatter and his knees won't stop trembling, he manages to call, 'What k-kind of p-presents do you want?'

'This mountain is very cold.' Awesome's shiver sends rocks tumbling down the mountain. 'I need a warm coat.'

Arthur quickly takes off his coat and hands it to the ogre, who stretches and stretches the coat until it fits him.

Then the ogre yells so the entire mountain range resounds with his voice, 'I'm hungry. What did you bring me to eat?'

Heart thumping like a drum, Draggle hands him their sandwiches and they disappear into Awesome's cavernous mouth.

'That's okay so far,' Awesome moans. 'But I'm so miserable. What can you do to make me laugh?'

Draggle puffs a little smoke and calls, 'What did the ogre do at the wedding?'

'He toasted the bride and the groom,' Arthur yells.

Awesome's laugh echoes through the mountains and valley.

Arthur takes heart from this. 'What happened when the ogre entered a beauty contest?'

'He came fourth and ate all the judges,' Draggle loudly snorts.

As they tell more jokes, and Awesome chortles and laughs, he begins to shrink.

'What happened to the football team when they played the ogres?' 'They got eaten alive.'

'How do ogres like their eggs?'

'Terror-fried.'

By now Awesome is laughing so hard, he's shrinking . . . shrinking . . . until he's only the size of a man.

Quick as a wink, Draggle holds him down with his strong tail. While he sends puffs of smoke into Awesome's eyes so he can't see, Arthur waves his sword over their captive in case he tries to

escape. This way they keep telling jokes, meanwhile watching Awesome laugh and laugh . . . and shrivel up and up to the size of a walnut until he finally . . . disappears.

Arthur and Draggle collect Awesome's treasure and carry it back home, where they claim the King's reward and use all that gold to repair both Castle Bravery and Dragon Cave to make them good as new.

But best by far is that no one dares tease or call them bad names ever again. Instead, they're known as Amazing Arthur and Daring Draggle.

SLUGS AND SNAILS

BY JENNY BLACKFORD

One afternoon while Alexis was
supposed to be minding her baby
brother Nicky, her cousin Eric fed him
a handful of fat, slimy slugs. Alexis tried
to pull Eric away from Nicky, but he was
bigger than her, and his skin had always
been slippery. Even when she grabbed
him hard, her hands slid right off.
It was hopeless.

As usual, *she* was the one who got into
trouble.

Her mother said, 'Alexis, why did
you let your cousin do that to your baby

brother? You're older than Eric; you should have known better.'

There was no point arguing. No one but Alexis knew what Eric was really like. Alexis just said, 'Sorry, Mum.'

But she couldn't understand why her mum was *so* upset. Nicky had hardly swallowed any of the slugs, really. He'd spat most of them straight out. And they were *organic* slugs. The family never used poisons on the garden, not even snail pellets.

But then Eric did something even worse.

It all started with his mother's strawberries. A few days after Aunty Vita promised the whole family her famous pavlova with masses of strawberries and cream on top, all the strawberries disappeared from her garden overnight. Whatever ate them even ate the leaves. All that was left in the strawberry patch was a tough-looking brown stalk or two coming up out of the ground. At the family barbecue that weekend, they had to have last year's frozen passionfruit on the pav.

After they'd finished the pavlova, and Eric had licked up all the crunchy crumbs while the grown-ups weren't looking, everybody went out to the backyard to look at what had happened to the strawberries.

Aunty Vita leaned against her big green rainwater tank while the rest of the family poked around in her strawberry patch. She was tall and thin, bleached-blonde and worried-looking; not at all like her son Eric, who was sort of rounded and brown and smug, with brown hair and bulgy brown eyes. (Alexis thought that Aunty Vita was probably worried-looking after all her years with Eric.)

Alexis could see her mum and dad smirking at one another, and she knew they were thinking about how bad Aunty Vita's strawberry bed looked, and how good the fruit on their apricot trees looked, over the fence. The fruit would be ripe in a few weeks, and they would all have a feast – and Alexis's parents would be one up on Aunty Vita.

'Poor Vita,' Alexis's mother said, shaking her long red hair.

'It's not so bad,' Aunty Vita said. 'I've still got the silverbeet, the zucchinis –'

Alexis's mother took no notice. She said, 'Oh, but how *awful* for you, Vita, to lose all your lovely strawberries, after you'd promised them to us and everything.'

Aunty Vita gave a smile that was a bit like a snarl. She said, 'It was full moon – maybe that had something to do with it. But even if there were hundreds of snails, could they really have eaten all those plants in one night?'

'Maybe. Look at all the snail trails,' Alexis's mother said, pointing.

There shouldn't have been *any* snails in Aunty Vita's garden. Alexis got most of her pocket money from collecting snails and slugs from the family backyards and taking them around the street to Poppa for his ducks to eat. She got paid per snail or slug, and she'd only found two snails in Aunty Vita's yard the last time, even though she'd looked *everywhere*.

Her grandfather was just watching and not saying anything. He looked worried, though.

'What do you think, Poppa?' she asked him quietly, in Italian. His English was fine, but it felt special, speaking Italian to him.

'If it was snails that ate those strawberries,' he said in a deep, serious voice, 'they must have been very big and very greedy. Take a good look.'

Alexis was a lot closer to the ground than the grown-ups, and she knelt down so she was even closer. It looked like just one, single, really wide snail trail. As Alexis looked up, her hands held half a metre apart, Poppa nodded. But the wrinkle between his bushy eyebrows grew even deeper.

Then he said, 'It was full moon last night.'

'What could that have to do with it?' Alexis asked, but he wouldn't say any more.

———

Eric went to sleep at school the next day, and Alexis wanted to fall through the floor when he started to snore. Living next door to him was bad enough, but being in the same class at school was

worse. But what could she do? After all, he was her cousin.

It was funny, though: Eric didn't seem upset about the strawberries disappearing, even though he was always so greedy.

Four weeks later, the same thing happened to the apricots. All the golden fruit, and even all the leaves, disappeared overnight, and there was silver snail slime over the trees. Mum and Dad didn't

smirk this time, but maybe Aunty Vita
didn't look quite sympathetic enough.
Eric smirked, though.

Typical, Alexis thought. She looked
at Poppa, who held his hands wide apart
and frowned. She knew what he meant –
ordinary garden snails couldn't have
done that. It must have been something
really big. But what?

'It was full moon again,' he said.

The day after the apricots
disappeared, Eric was looking so sleepy
and smug at school that Alexis knew
he'd soon be snoring. He looked even
rounder than usual, and his big brown
eyes looked bulgier than ever.

She usually tried not to touch him,
but it was better than having the whole

class stare at her when he started snoring. She leaned over the gap between them and shook him by the elbow.

Yuck! There was some weird sort of slime on his skin, and it came off on her fingers. She tried to wipe it off on her T-shirt, but her hand still felt all slimy. Eric really was disgusting.

Alexis started to wonder why the strawberries and the apricots had both disappeared at full moon. Could there be some weird sort of monster that only came out at full moon and gorged itself on fruit? But it couldn't be a werewolf – they ate meat, not fruit. And vampires drank blood.

Maybe it was a giant vampire fruit bat that only came out at full moon!

But she wasn't sure, because it didn't explain the snail trails.

The next full moon, Alexis had a plan. She thought it was going to be Aunty Vita's figs this time. It was Tuesday, which was the evening Aunty Vita went to her art class, so Eric had dinner with Alexis and her mum and dad, and baby Nicky. Alexis had seen Aunty Vita's paintings and thought that her aunt probably only went to the class to get away from Eric. As usual, Eric kicked Alexis's ankles under the table and yelled so much that he made poor baby Nicky scream and scream.

As soon as Aunty Vita finally came to pick up Eric, Alexis went to her bedroom. She put on jeans and a dark blue T-shirt and sneakers so she'd be hard to see in the dark, and sat in her chair near the window, watching. She was going to stay awake until eleven, when her parents should be asleep, and then she would sneak out and over the fence to see if anything happened to Aunty Vita's fig trees overnight – but she was really sleepy.

———

Alexis suddenly woke up in her chair and looked at the clock. It was 2 am.

Oh, no! She'd fallen asleep! The light of the full moon was coming straight through her window. Without turning the light on, Alexis sneaked out into the garden, up one of the apricot trees and over the fence to Aunty Vita's garden.

On the other side of the yard, the fig trees were stripped bare. Every fruit and leaf had been eaten. Silver slime glistened on the bare bark in the moonlight.

Alexis's plan had failed – she'd slept right through it. She'd missed whatever was eating the fruit during the full moon.

But Eric's window was wide open. Alexis walked over, very quietly, and looked in. There was no sign of Eric! What trouble was he up to this time, out of his room in the middle of the night? And would she get blamed for whatever he did?

She was just about to turn back when she noticed a wide, shiny trail on the windowsill. She stuck her head and

shoulders through the window, trying
to avoid touching the slimy windowsill,
to see where the trail led.

There was a huge, round, brown blob
up near the ceiling. Could it be a giant
fruit bat? No, it was much too round.
Alexis kept looking until her eyes got
used to the dark in the room.

It was a giant snail! And it looked just
like Eric, bulgy eyes and everything!

All at once, things fell into place.

It had to be *Eric* that was eating the
fruit. Alexis's round, slimy cousin was

a were-snail. At full moon, he slid out through his window and went hunting.

Alexis stood with her head and shoulders inside Eric's window, gazing up at the giant snail. Her mouth was hanging open. What could she do? There was no point telling Mum and Dad, or Aunty Vita. They would *never* believe her. And she couldn't use snail pellets to keep Eric out of the family's gardens. He was her cousin, after all.

Suddenly, Alexis felt a gentle tap on her back. She jumped and hit her shoulder on the frame of the open window. She almost screamed, but she could hear someone saying 'Shhh' very quietly. Then the person said, 'It's all right, Alexis. It's just me, Poppa.'

She let out a huge breath and pulled her head out of the window. 'What are you doing here?' she whispered.

Poppa pointed through the window. 'It's your cousin Eric. He's a –' but then he stopped.

'He's a were-snail?' Alexis asked.

Poppa sighed. 'Yes. My mother told me about them when I was your age. There used to be some around her village, back in Italy. She said they were not as dangerous as werewolves, but still not good to have around.'

'Should we be standing here talking about him?' Alexis said. 'Won't he hear us?'

'Your cousin is fast asleep now, I think. After he ate all those figs, he'll find it very hard to stay awake.'

151

That made sense. It explained why he'd kept going to sleep at school. 'But we shouldn't hang around here for too long. What if Aunty Vita wakes up and finds us here?'

Poppa nodded. 'You're right. Can you see me after school tomorrow? We have to protect my plums next full moon.'

———

Alexis could hardly wait to get to Poppa's place. She wriggled in her seat all afternoon. As soon as the bell rang, she raced off.

Poppa worked from home as an accountant. When Alexis ran around the corner into his driveway, he was just saying goodbye to one of his

clients. Alexis said a polite hello to Mrs
Papadopoulos, but she was too excited
to concentrate on anything until she was
sitting alone with Poppa in his den at the
back of the house.

Poppa had a pile of white bulbs on
the coffee table. He pointed to them,
and said, 'There's our secret weapon.'

'Garlic?' she said.

'Yes, garlic. My mother told me that
it works against all of the supernatural
creatures: vampires, werewolves, even
were-snails.'

'Cool,' Alexis said. But something
was worrying her. 'But, Poppa, Eric eats
garlic all the time. We'll have to come up
with something else. A moat around the
fruit trees maybe . . .'

'Ah,' Poppa said seriously. 'Garlic can't hurt Eric when he's a *boy*. But when he turns into a snail, it will work.'

'So what do we do?'

In the following weeks, Poppa and Alexis laboured on their secret plan. Their families didn't notice. They thought they were just working in the garden, as usual.

In the first week, Poppa and Alexis split big papery garlic bulbs into handfuls of single cloves and put them in a bucket. Next, they used a wooden dibber to make holes about a hand's width apart around the edge of every single fruit or vegetable bed in all the family's gardens. Then Alexis put one of the garlic cloves from the bucket into each of the holes, pointy side up, and filled in the hole with soil. Poppa followed her around with a watering can filled from his old steel rainwater tank.

By the following week, little green shoots were appearing all around the edges of the garden beds. Alexis went around each of the gardens every afternoon to make sure that the baby garlic plants were growing and that nothing was eating them.

Next, they mixed a special batch of Poppa's garlic mixture, which he usually sprayed onto his tomato plants to keep the bugs away. They mashed up a whole lot of garlic – ten big heads of it – in a big glass jar and poured boiling water over it, and left it to sit for a week. When

Poppa opened the jar, it smelled almost as bad as Nicky's nappies, but different. They emptied it into a big bucket and topped it up with water from his tank.

Instead of spraying the garlic mixture onto leaves, they used clean paintbrushes to paint it around the trunks of all the fruit trees, from ground level up to Alexis's height. They paid special attention to Poppa's plum trees, which were practically bursting with purple fruit.

On the day of the full moon, just to be sure, they climbed up into the plum trees and hung garlic cloves all over the branches on bits of string.

'I think we're prepared for anything, now,' said Poppa. 'I'll come to your window after your parents turn the lights off.'

A bit after eleven that night, Alexis and Poppa were standing under his grapevine, watching his plum trees. The full moon was high above them. It gave a silvery gleam to the skins of the fat purple fruit hanging from the trees.

Poppa nudged Alexis and pointed. A huge snail, the size of Eric, was making its slimy way towards the trees. Alexis could see the snail's muscular brown foot rippling as it propelled the big round shell along the ground. It left a wide silver trail that glistened in the moonlight.

Soon the front of the snail's foot touched the base of the closest plum tree and wriggled its way upwards. In no time, the huge snail was hanging off the tree, about as high up as Alexis's shoulders.

Suddenly, the were-snail dropped back onto the mulch under the tree, upside down, with its slimy brown foot wiggling around in the air.

'What's happening?' Alexis whispered to Poppa.

'Just watch,' he said.

The snail writhed and wriggled. Green slime bubbled out of the wet-looking surface of its foot. Alexis swallowed. The snail kept writhing, until it suddenly turned into – Eric!

He looked up at Poppa and Alexis,

guiltily. 'It wasn't me,' he said. 'It was Alexis's fault.'

'Don't be silly, Eric,' Poppa told him. 'You're not going to get away with that this time. We saw everything.'

'It's not true. I'm *not* a were-snail,' Eric said.

'Rubbish,' Poppa said firmly. 'There's only one thing you can do.'

'What?' Eric said, in a nasty voice.

'Stay inside on full-moon nights. Keep your window closed and your blind down. That will keep you safe.'

'But *I'm* not in any danger,' Eric said. 'It's just a bit of fun.'

'If you get squashed by someone who doesn't know who you are, it won't be much fun,' said Poppa.

Eric looked sulky. 'That's not going to happen.'

Poppa said, 'Promise me, Eric, or I'll tell your mother.'

'You wouldn't.' But then Eric looked less sure. 'Would you?'

Poppa just nodded.

'Alexis, you wouldn't let him, would you?' said Eric.

Alexis smiled. 'What do you think, Eric?'

———

On the weekend, Poppa held a barbecue for the whole family. They had lamb chops with tomato sauce, and chicken marinated with basil and olive oil, and fish cooked in foil with lemon and garlic, plus lots of fresh salad from Poppa's garden. Afterwards, there were Alexis's mother's plum tarts and Aunty Vita's pavlova with poached plums and cream, as well as a pile of Poppa's fresh plums on a big plate in the centre of the table. Masses of big purple plums still hung from the branches.

While everyone was busy eating and drinking, Poppa gently nudged Alexis in the ribs and nodded his head towards Eric, who was shovelling plum tart into his mouth with one hand and pavlova with the other.

'It's just as well we caught Eric,' Poppa said.

'Or we wouldn't have had any plums?' said Alexis.

'No,' Poppa said, very seriously.
'He might have eaten so much that his
shell burst!'

The picture sprung to Alexis's mind.
The garden would have been covered in
slimy splattered bits of giant snail! Ew!

Alexis looked at Eric, still stuffing
food into his mouth, then looked back
at Poppa, and started to laugh.

CLEMENTINE ROSE AND THE VERY EARLY START

JACQUELINE HARVEY

FIRST DAY

Clementine Rose pushed back the bed covers and slipped down onto the cool wooden floor. A full moon hung low in the sky, lighting up pockets of the garden outside and casting a yellow glow over her room. Somewhere, a shutter was banging in the breeze, keeping time like a drummer in a marching band. But that's not what woke Clementine up. She was used to the noises of Penberthy House. It talked to her all the time.

Clementine tiptoed to the end of her bed and knelt down. She rested her head on Lavender's tummy but the little pig was fast asleep in her basket. Her shallow breaths were interrupted every now and then by a snorty grunt.

'I'd better get dressed,' Clementine whispered. 'I don't want to be late on the first day.'

Clementine skipped over to her wardrobe. Hanging on the door was her favourite new outfit. There was a pretty pink and white checked tunic, white socks and red shoes. Clementine especially adored the red blazer with swirly letters embroidered on the pocket. It was her new school uniform, which she had insisted on wearing around the house for the past week. Clementine had packed and repacked her schoolbag for almost a month too.

Clementine wriggled out of her pyjamas and got dressed, buckling her shoes last of all. She brushed her hair and pinned it off her face with a red bow. She smiled at her reflection in the mirror.

'Very smart,' she whispered to
herself, just as Mrs Mogg had done when
Clementine had appeared at the village
store in her uniform the day before.
Clementine glanced at her pet, who
hadn't moved a muscle. She decided
to let Lavender sleep in and headed
downstairs to find her mother and
Uncle Digby.

On the way, she stopped to chat
with her grandparents. Well, with the
portraits of her grandparents that hung
on the wall.

'Good morning, Granny and
Grandpa. Today's that big day I was
telling you all about yesterday and the
day before and the day before that.
I can't wait. I'll get to play with Sophie

and Poppy and I'm going to learn how to read and do numbers and tell the time. Did you like school?' She peered up at her grandfather. She could have sworn he nodded his head ever so slightly.

'What about you, Granny?' She looked at the portrait of her grandmother dressed in a splendid gown, with the Appleby diamond tiara on her head. She wore the matching necklace and earrings too. Everyone had thought the jewellery was lost until Aunt Violet had found it when she came to stay. Now the tiara and earrings were safely hidden away in the vault while her mother decided what to do with them; the necklace was still missing. Uncle Digby said that if the jewellery was sold it would bring enough money to pay for a new roof, which Penberthy House badly needed. But Lady Clarissa said that she would wait a while to decide. The roof had leaked for years and they were used to putting the buckets out, so there was no hurry.

Clementine studied her grandmother's expression. There was just a hint of a lovely smile. She took that to mean that she had enjoyed school too.

Clementine looked at the next portrait along, which showed a beautiful young woman. Clementine had called her Grace until, to her surprise, her Great-Aunt Violet had arrived at the house a few months ago and revealed that she was the woman in the painting.

Clementine was shocked to learn that the woman was still alive because everyone else in the pictures was long gone.

Aunt Violet and Clementine hadn't exactly hit it off when they first met but for now the old woman was away on a world cruise, so Clementine didn't have to worry about her. Sooner or later, though, she'd be back.

Uncle Digby always said that a day at the seaside would cheer anyone up. So Clementine thought Aunt Violet should be the happiest person on earth by the time she returned from her cruise. When she had told her mother and Uncle Digby that, they had both laughed and said that they hoped very much that she was right.

Downstairs in the hallway, the ancient grandfather clock began to chime. Clemmie always thought it sounded sad.

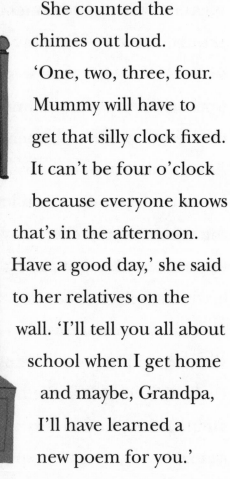

She counted the chimes out loud.

'One, two, three, four. Mummy will have to get that silly clock fixed. It can't be four o'clock because everyone knows that's in the afternoon. Have a good day,' she said to her relatives on the wall. 'I'll tell you all about school when I get home and maybe, Grandpa, I'll have learned a new poem for you.'

Ever since Clemmie could talk, Uncle Digby had taught her poems, which she loved to recite. She often performed for guests who came to stay too, and even though she couldn't yet read, she had a wonderful memory.

Clementine bounced down the stairs and along the hallway to the kitchen. It was still in darkness. Pharaoh, Aunt Violet's sphynx cat, was asleep in his basket beside the stove.

'Mummy and Uncle Digby must be having a sleep-in, like Lavender and Pharaoh,' Clementine said to herself. She hoped they would be up soon.

The little girl climbed onto the stool in the pantry and pulled out a box of cereal, set a bowl and a spoon on the

table and fetched the milk from the
fridge.

She managed to pour her breakfast
without spilling too much. Thankfully,
none landed on her uniform.

Clementine listened to the sounds
of the house as she ate. Sometimes
when people came to stay they asked
her mother if Penberthy House had any
ghosts. Most children Clemmie's age
would have been frightened by the idea,
but she often imagined her grandfather
and grandmother coming to life at
night-time, stepping out of their
paintings and having tea in the sitting
room, or drifting through the halls.

Clementine swallowed the last
spoonful of cereal. 'Good,' she said to

herself. 'Now I can go as soon as Mummy
and . . . Uncle Digby . . .' Her eyelids
drooped and she yawned loudly.

She rested her head on the table and
within a minute she was fast asleep.

TIME TO GO

'Clemmie.' Lady Clarissa gently stroked
her daughter's hair. 'Wake up, sleepyhead.'

Clementine's face crumpled and
she struggled to open her eyes until she
remembered what day it was and sat bolt
upright.

'Did I miss it?' she asked.

'Miss what?' her mother replied.

'School, of course.' Clementine
sniffed. She could smell toast cooking.

'No, Clemmie, it's just after seven.'
Her mother shook her head. 'How long
have you been up?'

'I don't know. The clock chimed four
times but it must be broken because
that's in the afternoon,' Clementine
explained.

'Oh dear, you've been up for hours, silly sausage. I hope you're not too tired for your first day.' Lady Clarissa put a plate of hot buttery toast with strawberry jam in front of her daughter. 'Four o'clock can be in the morning too, Clemmie, and it's very early – at least three hours before you usually get up.'

'Oh.' Clementine frowned. 'Well, today I'll learn how to tell the time and then I won't get up too early tomorrow.'

Digby Pertwhistle arrived in the kitchen. He had been the butler at Penberthy House for longer than anyone could remember and was more like a beloved uncle to Clarissa and Clementine than an employee. He and

Clarissa ran the house as a country hotel, but unfortunately guests were few and far between.

'Good morning, Clementine. Are you all ready for the big day?' he asked, his grey eyes twinkling.

'Oh yes, Uncle Digby,' said Clementine, nodding. 'I've been ready forever.'

Digby and Clarissa smiled at one another. That was certainly true.

'Well, eat up your toast and drink your juice. You'll need lots of energy. I've packed your morning tea and I think –' her mother opened the lid of the red lunchbox which had Clementine's name written neatly on the lid – 'Uncle Digby has added a treat.' She snapped the lid closed again.

The old man winked at Clementine. She tried to wink back but she just double blinked instead.

'I've got the camera ready,' said Digby. He walked over to the sideboard and picked up a small black bag.

'Goody!' said Clementine. She finished the last bite of her toast and jumped down from the chair. 'I'll just get Lavender ready. She had a sleep-in.'

'Clemmie, I don't know if we can take her with us today,' said her mother. 'I'm not sure how the school feels about pets.'

'But I told her she could come. Please,' Clementine begged her mother.

Pharaoh let out a loud meow as he stood up in his basket and arched his back.

'No, Pharaoh, you are definitely not coming. Can you imagine what would happen if we took you to town and you got away?' Digby shook his head.

'We don't want to make Aunt Violet cross again, that's for sure,' Clementine replied. 'But Lavender will be so sad if she has to stay home. She's been looking forward to school for as long as I have.'

'Well, what about if I take care of Lavender when you and your mother go into school,' Digby suggested. 'We can go for a walk around the village and I can pop into the patisserie and see Pierre.'

'And you can get a great big cream bun for your morning tea!' Clementine announced.

'Oh, I haven't had one of Pierre's cream buns for ages.' Digby's stomach gurgled at the thought of it.

'All right, now run along, Clemmie, and brush your teeth. We'll have to leave soon,' her mother instructed.

Clementine skipped up the back stairs to her room on the third floor, singing to herself on the way, 'I get to go to school today, I can't wait, hip hip hooray . . .'

ABOUT THE AUTHORS

BELINDA MURRELL has worked as a travel journalist, technical medical writer and public relations consultant. Her overseas adventures inspired her travel writing, which has appeared in newspapers such as *The Sydney Morning Herald*. Although she studied Children's Literature at Macquarie University, her passion for children's books was truly reignited when she had her own three children and began telling them stories and writing them down. Belinda's books include the Sun Sword trilogy and a number of evocative timeslip tales, such as *Locket of Dreams* and *The Forgotten Pearl*. Belinda's books are so loved by children that they have been shortlisted for many prestigious awards and her Lulu Bell series is a particular favourite with her young readers. She is an Author Ambassador for Room to Read. Visit her website at www.belindamurrell.com.au

BILL CONDON It has long been rumoured that Bill Condon is a vampire or a werewolf. The truth is that he just looks like a monster because he is very old. He is so old that even his wrinkles have wrinkles!

However, he still manages to keep feeling young by writing stories. That never fails to make him happy. In 2010 he won the Prime Minister's Literary Award for young adult fiction. Bill's latest novel for junior readers is *The Simple Things*, published in 2014. He lives on the south coast of New South Wales with his wife, the well-known children's author Dianne Bates. Visit Bill at his website www.enterprisingwords.com.au

CELESTE WALTERS has taught children in primary school and grown-ups at university. She has published texts, poetry and novels – her latest, *A Certain Music*, having been deemed a Vintage Classic. At the family farm Celeste reads to the chooks, tests ideas on the alpacas, feeds motherless lambs and tiptoes past the bulls. She thinks a farm is the best for watching stories unfold, as illustrated in *Little Lambchops*. Another story involved spiriting a lamb back to the city to save a dad from eternally mowing the grass. But that's another story . . .

DAVID HARDING enjoys writing 'grinking' stories – ones that make kids grin while they think. He's a primary school teacher who lives and runs in and around Sydney with his wife and two sons. Besides writing books for the RSPCA Animal Tales series and the Robert Irwin, Dinosaur Hunter series, both published by Random House Australia, David has written books in another bestselling Australian series for boys and is a regular contributor to *The School Magazine* (NSW).

FIONA MCDONALD The first big book Fiona read was *The Lion, the Witch and the Wardrobe* by C. S. Lewis, and she immediately started trying to find Narnia. However, as she grew up Fiona realised this could only be done through stories. When she was 21 she went to art school and learnt to draw. A few years later she moved to the magical Blue Mountains and began a career as a doll and dragon maker. A bit later on Fiona went to university to study English and Italian literature. It was while she was doing this that she fell in love with the medieval Italian poet Dante Alighieri. Finally, when she became a grandmother, Fiona decided to search for Narnia again and began writing seriously. She now has twelve books published in the US and the UK. She has one children's novel, *Ghost Doll and Jasper,* published by Sky Pony Press.

GRACE ATWOOD is a freelance editor and writer who loves stories of all kinds. She lives in Sydney with her family and a slightly unhinged silver Bengal cat. She doesn't like sharks as much as Charlie but she does love aquariums, travel and Moroccan donkeys. Her first picture book, *Meet Nancy Bird Walton*, illustrated by Harry Slaghekke, was published by Random House Australia in 2014.

GEORGE IVANOFF is an author and stay-at-home dad residing in Melbourne. He has written over 70 books for children and teenagers, and is best known for his You Choose interactive books and Gamers novels. He has books on both the Victorian and NSW Premier's Reading Challenge lists, and he has won a couple of awards that no one has heard of. George has also had stories published in numerous magazines and anthologies, including *Trust Me Too, Stories for Girls* and *Stories for Boys.* George drinks too much coffee, eats too much chocolate and watches too much *Doctor Who.* If you'd like to find out more about George and his writing, check out his website at www.georgeivanoff.com.au

SOPHIE MASSON Born in Indonesia of French parents, Sophie Masson is the author of more than 50 novels for children, young adults and adults, published in Australia and internationally. Her historical novel *The Hunt for Ned Kelly* won the Patricia Wrightson Prize for Children's Literature in the 2011 NSW Premier's Literary Awards. Her more recent novels are the young adult fairytale *Moonlight and Ashes* and the fantasy adventure for younger readers *The Boggle Hunters*. Her short stories have been published in many anthologies, including *30 Australian Stories for Children*. Her website is www.sophiemasson.org

VASHTI FARRER writes for adults and children. She has had over 60 short stories for adults published, won five major awards and has written 26 books for children. Her love of history has meant that a good deal of her work is history based, covering a wide range of topics. Her latest book, *Ellen Thomson: Beyond a Reasonable Doubt?*, is her first non-fiction book for adults, based on a murder which took place in north Queensland in 1886. An article she wrote called 'The Only Woman', based on the case, won the non-fiction section of the inaugural New England Thunderbolt prize for Crime Writing in 2013. Visit Vashti at www.vashtifarrer.com

GOLDIE ALEXANDER's 80 books are published both here and overseas. Her novels for adults include *The Grevillea Murder Mystery Trilogy* and *Penelope's Ghost* plus many prize-winning short stories and articles. For children, she is best known for *My Australian Story: Surviving Sydney Cove*, which is now in its eleventh edition. Her latest works for young readers include the A–Z PI Mystery series, plus three collections of short stories: *Killer Virus*,

Horrible Cousins and *Space Footy*. For young adults there are *That Stranger Next Door, In Hades, Dessi's Romance* and *The Youngest Cameleer*. For middle grade readers, Goldie has written *eSide: A Journey into Cyberspace, Neptunia* and *Cybertricks*; and for young readers: *Galipolli Medals*. Her non-fiction includes *Mentoring Your Memoir*, which she uses to facilitate creative writing workshops. She also mentors many emerging authors. Visit Goldie at www.goldiealexander.com

JENNY BLACKFORD is a writer and poet interested in science fiction and fantasy, ancient history and religion, food, gardening, and the natural world. She writes novels, stories and poems of all sorts of genres, from serious to spooky, for children, YA readers and adults. In 2001, she started writing full-time. Her historical novel *The Priestess and the Slave* was published in 2009, the year that she and her husband (and their ragdoll cat, Felix) moved back home to Newcastle. In 2013 Jenny published an illustrated collection of cat poems called *The Duties of a Cat*.

JACQUELINE HARVEY has spent much of her working life teaching in girls' boarding schools. Her bestselling Alice-Miranda series has been a runaway success in Australia and has also been published internationally to great acclaim. She is pleased to say that she has never yet encountered a headmistress like her character, Miss Grimm, but she has come across quite a few girls who remind her a little of Alice-Miranda. Jacqueline has also published an increasingly popular series for younger readers featuring an adorable five-year-old girl called Clementine Rose, proud owner of Lavender, a teacup pig. Visit Jacqueline's website at www.jacquelineharvey.com.au

ABOUT THE EDITOR

Linsay Knight is widely respected as a leading expert in, and contributor to, children's literature in Australia. As former Head of Children's Books at Random House Australia, she nurtured the talent of numerous authors and illustrators to create some of Australia's most successful children's books. Linsay is also a lexicographer, having written and edited many dictionaries and thesauruses, is the author of a number of successful non-fiction books for children and adults, and the editor of a number of story collections, including *30 Australian Stories for Children*, *30 Australian Ghost Stories for Children* and two series of age-story collections like this one.

ABOUT THE ILLUSTRATOR

Tom Jellett has illustrated a number of books for children, including *Australia at the Beach* by Max Fatchen, The Littlest Pirate series by Sherryl Clark for Penguin Books, *The Gobbledygook is Eating a Book* by Justine Clarke and Arthur Baysting, *My Dad Thinks He's Funny* by Katrina Germein and the follow up *My Dad Still Thinks He's Funny* for Walker Books. Tom has also been included in the Editorial and Book category for the Society of Illustrators Annual Exhibition, New York in 2013 and 2014. He was also included in Communication Arts Illustration Annual 2012, 3×3 Children's Show No. 9, 10 and 11, and was Highly Commended in the 2013 Illustrators Australia Awards. For more information about Tom and his work visit www.tomjellett.com

ACKNOWLEDGEMENTS

'Lulu Bell and the Beach Adventure' from *Lulu Bell and the Fairy Penguin* by Belinda Murrell, first published by Random House Australia in 2013. Text copyright © Belinda Murrell 2013.

'That's Showbiz' by Bill Condon first published by Random House Australia in 2014. Text copyright © Bill Condon 2014.

'Little Lambchops' by Celeste Walters first published by Random House Australia in 2014. Text copyright © Celeste Walters 2014.

'Scary Fairies' by David Harding first published by Random House Australia in 2014. Text copyright © David Harding 2014.

'The Goblin Princess' by Fiona McDonald first published by Random House Australia in 2014. Text copyright © Fiona McDonald 2014.

'Charlie and Lou the Shark' by Grace Atwood first published by Random House Australia in 2014. Text copyright © Grace Atwood 2014.

'The Dog Ate My Homework' by George Ivanoff first published in *The School Magazine* (2006), vol. 91.1. Text copyright © Geroge Ivanoff 2006.

LOOK OUT FOR THESE OTHER GREAT STORY COLLECTIONS

OUT NOW